Graves are robbed, barns are set on fire, a boat is overturned and a child nearly drowns, and a man is attacked and hanged in his own house. Enraged townspeople blame Stan Parker, the lonely man who lives in the eerie manor house on bleak Cornwall Crag and has strange attacks of madness when the moon is full. James and Honey, however, suspect that things may not be what they seem—and risk their own lives to solve THE MYSTERY OF THE MADMAN AT CORNWALL CRAG.

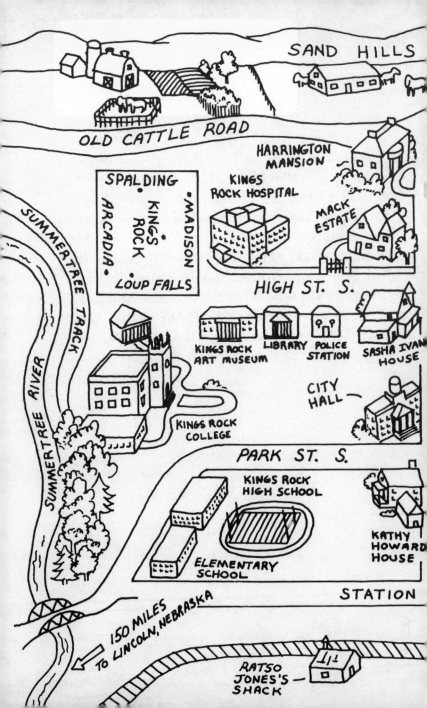

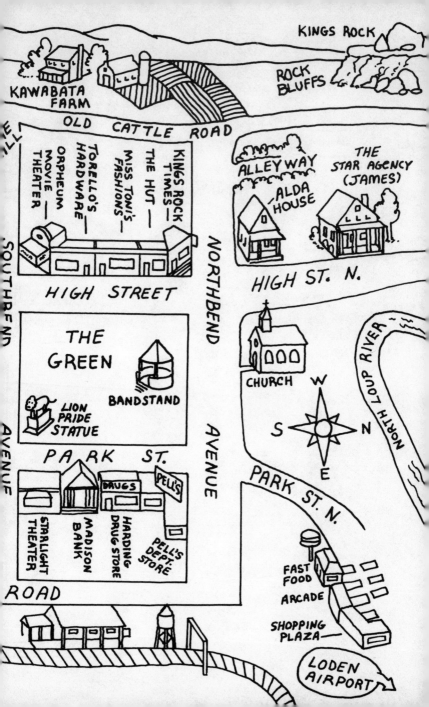

JAMES BUDD

1

JAMES BUDD
1

THE MYSTERY OF THE
MADMAN AT CORNWALL CRAG

By Dale Carlson

Illustrated by
Tom LaPadula

Cover illustration by
Chuck Liese

A GOLDEN BOOK · NEW YORK
WESTERN PUBLISHING COMPANY, INC.
RACINE, WISCONSIN 53404

For Stan Park, my husband
A strong, gentle man
And my love always

Contents

1. Robbed Graves   13
2. The Haunting Crag   21
3. The Madman   28
4. The Madman Disappears   35
5. Hands Dripping Blood   46
6. Stan Parker's Secret   54
7. Liz's Secret   66
8. Ghost on the Prairie   73
9. Danger in the Mists   79
10. Skeletons in a Crypt   87
11. Dead or Alive?   94
12. Honey Is Missing   102
13. Ratso Plays a Part   108
14. Sam on the Scene   116
15. Locked in the Crypt   125
16. Future Plans—and Pillows   136

THE MYSTERY OF THE
MADMAN AT
CORNWALL
CRAG

CHAPTER ONE

Robbed Graves

Another grave had just been robbed.

"Get James," the graveyard caretaker had said in a hoarse, frightened voice. "Get James Budd. He'll know what to do. That young man always knows what to do."

As James left the car, in the darkening September afternoon, to climb toward the old graveyard, he saw a skulking form against the sky. As soon as James came close, it disappeared from view.

"Who's there?" James called out sharply. But there was no reply.

An old graveyard—with the wind coming off the empty Nebraska plains and sighing gustily among the tombs, like the lingering sounds of the dead—was really, thought James, nowhere to be with night coming on.

He moved through the moldering, moss-covered headstones. He could see, near the edge of the graveyard, the newly dug-up coffin, ripped from the earth and tilted crazily against the sky. He knew from the police report that the contents of the coffin were gone.

James Budd, at sixteen, was not only the adopted son of the famous private detective Sam Star, but also his right-hand man at the Star Agency. Besides taking on private cases, they often assisted Sam's old friend, Police Chief Frank Adams. After school, during vacations, and whenever Sam was away on a case, James worked for or took over for Sam. People in Kings Rock, and all over Nebraska and the Midwest, were as accustomed to seeing James Budd on a case as Sam Star.

"James is a born fixer," Sam often said. "He can't leave well enough, or anything else, alone. And if there's no trouble to fix," he would add, "leave it to James, he'll make some."

"James?" Honey Mack's voice called out.

She had ridden up on her blue Honda CB125S from the offices of the Star Agency, where James had left her the note Sam had left for him: *Call Chief Adams re: coffins. Handle case till I get back Friday.* James had simply added: *Meet me old graveyard. J.*

"I'm not crazy about it up here, James," Honey said in a quavery voice.

James grinned. He put an arm around Honey's slender waist, touching the waist-long, honey-gold hair that gave Honey her name. Honey Mack was more than the prettiest girl in Kings Rock High School's junior class. She was also the fastest runner, the fastest—and best—driver, and, best of all, James was occasionally heard to say, "She's my girl." Honey worked for Sam Star, too, and wrote up their cases, often for publication in the *Kings Rock Times*.

"This graveyard is straight out of Edgar Allan Poe," James agreed.

But Honey had calmed down a little. After all, James Budd was here. She was tall, but even she had to look up at James—and she did so adoringly. In her opinion, and in the opinion of most of the females she knew, James Budd was the handsomest creation Nebraska had ever produced.

James was dark and clean-cut, with a strong jaw, wide, dark eyes, and black hair. He was not violent by nature, but he was a stubborn fighter for what he felt was right. He knew basic judo and karate, the arts of unarmed self-defense, in case of necessity; he bore a two-inch scar on his tanned forehead from an old fight. He was not only good-looking. He was also an all-round athlete and a straight-A student, and he liked to dress well. People around Kings Rock often remarked, when they saw James and Honey together, that the two made an elegant, well-matched couple.

"Do you think we could go make an elegant, well-matched couple somewhere else?" Honey asked James now.

"Just huddle into that sweater and give me another minute," said James. "I want to have a look at that coffin."

James crossed the overgrown graves to examine the evidence.

"James, don't walk on those graves," yelled Honey. "The dead will rise and haunt you."

"Right," said James, unconcerned. "Now will you please hold this flashlight?"

"James, where are you?" Honey yelped.

She rushed over, circling the moldy headstones to where James had been and now suddenly wasn't.

"Down here," said James. "Aim the light at this end of the coffin down here."

Honey held the flashlight where James pointed. In the bottom of the coffin was a dark blue muffler.

"Grave robber left us a message," said James. "Thoughtful."

"James, what kind of lunatic would open three graves on three successive nights?" Honey asked.

"What kind of lunatic would empty the coffins of their bones?" asked James. "And why? These weren't recent burials, either. It couldn't have been too pleasant, handling those bones."

"Do you suppose there was anything valuable in those coffins?" asked Honey.

"Chief Adams is investigating the records to find out whatever he can about the people who were buried in the coffins and the circumstances of the burials," said James. "But my guess is that these graves weren't robbed for anything valuable."

"That's my James, independent thinker," teased Honey.

"Born independent, remember?" said James, winking.

James's teasing remarks about being "born independent" were the only way he ever spoke of being orphaned by parents he never knew and being adopted at the age of four out of an orphanage by Sam Star.

Sam, Honey, and Charlie Alda, the electronics genius of their class and James's best friend, were James's family now. The only other family member was James's 1971 red Pontiac Firebird, almost totally rebuilt by Charlie, and James's most beloved possession.

James was walking Honey toward the Firebird now. "Can't see much more tonight," he said. "Might as well head back to town."

"Why are you shouting?" whispered Honey.

James whipped around. As he'd expected, the figure who had been skulking about earlier reappeared on the crest of the hill. Then, as James turned, the skulker quickly dropped into an open grave to hide. As James raced back, the figure jumped out, scrambled for the trees beyond the crest, and disappeared into the shadows.

"No use now," said James. "Come on. Leave the Honda. We'll take my car."

James drove down from the Sand Hills,

down Old Cattle Road, over to High Street, and on to the Star Agency.

After James had put the car in the garage, he and Honey ran up the front steps and into the hall. Whether it was the sudden chill of the autumn air or the unearthly chill of terror they had both felt in the graveyard that made them run, they were glad to be indoors.

To the left of the front hall was Sam and James's large leather-and-brass living room. The bedrooms were upstairs, the kitchen and Sam's rose garden in the back. To the right were the Star Agency's offices. James went through the waiting room into the back consultation office to make a phone call to Sam. Honey quickly picked up the mail in the front office and followed him. She didn't want to be alone too long.

The sudden jangling of the telephone made Honey jump.

James picked it up.

The woman's voice screaming at the other end was loud enough for even Honey to hear.

"Hurry! Hurry, please! It's the madman again. It's the madman of Cornwall Crag!"

CHAPTER TWO

The Haunting Crag

"We're on our way," said James.

"Who was that?" Honey asked when he'd hung up. "And we're on our way where?"

"That was Mrs. Jarko, the old woman who lives in the cottage near Cornwall Crag," said James. "She said her rabbits have been stolen. She blames it on Stanley Parker—the madman, as she calls him—and she wants us to do something."

"Do something? You bet we'll do something," said Honey. "It's bad enough when people torment each other. Hurting animals is inexcusable."

If James Budd protected the defenseless, Honey Mack nurtured them. "Picks up a stray a day" was how James described his partner.

As they were about to leave, the telephone rang again. James hesitated, then picked it up.

"This is Mrs. Evans," said the woman at the other end. "I am the nurse-housekeeper to Mr. Stanley Parker of Cornwall Crag. I've been hearing reports of trouble—robbed graves, stolen animals—trouble that is being laid at my employer's doorstep." Under her good manners, Mrs. Evans sounded upset. "I wonder," she said tentatively, "if I might retain the services of the Star Agency on behalf of Mr. Parker."

"I'm James Budd, Mrs. Evans, Mr. Star's assistant," said James. "Mr. Star is out of the country at the moment. But I'll be there as soon as I can for a preliminary investigation."

James's tone conveyed a reassuring combination of authority and concern for Mrs. Evans's welfare. Mrs. Evans was relieved and grateful. "I'll see you shortly, then, Mr. Budd," she said.

"Grab your notebook, you gorgeous Watson," said James to Honey. "We're off, first to hear Mrs. Jarko's complaints against Mr. Parker, then to Cornwall Crag to hear the defense."

Though they were going to travel north,
James first drove south, toward the Green at
the center of town. From the Green sprang
all of Kings Rock's streets—Northbend and
Southbend Avenues going east and west,
High Street and Park Street going north and
south. To the northwest, at the foot of the
Sand Hills, was Rock Bluffs, with the rock
plateau called Kings Rock—James's favorite
place, and the place that gave the town its
name. To the northeast were the shopping
malls, arcades, junk food row, and Loden Airport. To the east was the railroad; to the south
was Summertree River, flowing into Middle
Loup River. To the west stretched the farms,
the cornfields, and the cattle herds of Nebraska.

As they drove, James, as always, made
mental notes even of the familiar, filing any
small changes for future reference. "I feel
out of control unless I know where everything is," James often said.

They drove around the Green, past the
church, past Pell's Department Store, the
Madison Bank, the Starlight Movie Theater,
around past City Hall, up past Torello's Hardware Store and The Hut, where the gang

from school ate pizza, played video games, and hung out. James glanced at the Lion Pride statue at the south end of the Green, and at the old-fashioned bandstand at the north end. He felt that he was looking at the last normal things he would see for a while.

"There's something unholy about this case," he said. "I feel it already."

"Robbed graves, stolen animals, and a madman up at that weird place would ruffle even you, I should think," said Honey.

James was known for never getting ruffled, looking ruffled, or admitting to a ruffle even when he felt it.

The sound of church bells and the low wail of a train whistle accompanied them out of town.

Cornwall Crag was half an hour northwest of Kings Rock. James drove past the Kawabata farm, where he and Honey and their friends learned martial arts and meditation, and past Rock Bluffs. Then, as the night closed in, they came to a place shunned by most people, not only because of the whispered stories about the madman, but because the place itself was barren, and rather frightening even by day. It was as if the scrub and the marshes and the wild weeds and grass, even the stones of the forbidding house, held something unhealthy.

"Look up there, on the knoll," said James.

As Honey looked she felt a creeping sensation along her spine. There, rising above a low mist, was Cornwall Crag, the lonely stone manor house that was the symbol of Stanley Parker's lands, his life, and, more recently, his madness. Here, except for Mrs. Evans and Mr. Painter, his gardener and chauffeur, Stanley Parker lived alone, surrounded on one side by Rock Bluffs and on the other three sides by his vast estate. He was the last of the Parkers living in this ancient house, brought over stone by stone from Cornwall, England, four generations ago by Sir Stanley, tenth earl of Parker.

"How old do you think Mr. Parker would be now?" Honey asked.

James thought about the gossip he'd heard around town, and what Sam and Chief Adams had told him. "He'd have to be in his mid-thirties," he said.

Sam had said that Stan Parker, a Vietnam War veteran, had a gentle mind, unsuited for killing, and that he had cracked under the strain—not so much of being wounded, as of wounding others. After his time in the navy, serving in the Mekong Delta, he had spent a number of years in mental institutions. He suffered from "attacks" of madness, it was said, especially when the moon was full. During those periods, he had to be forcibly restrained and locked up, as he was considered dangerous to himself and others.

"Do you believe all that?" Honey asked.

James pulled the Firebird to a stop in front of the tiny cottage at the foot of the knoll, where old Mrs. Jarko lived.

"How about suspending judgment for a while, now that we're on the case?" said James. "Yesterday, I might have said maybe. Today, we've been hired to investigate. I'd rather hold off believing anything, and start from the beginning."

Honey apologetically put away her journalist's sense of drama. "You're right, James, of course," she said.

They were about to enter the tiny cottage when they were stopped in their tracks.

From the manor house high on the crag came a sound like the howl of an animal in pain. In the same instant, a single yellow light flickered on in an upstairs window.

A moment later, the window was flung open. In the yellow light, James and Honey could see the madman, arms flung wide, shrieking out his soul to the night sky. Whether he was communing with the darkness, or about to leap to his death in the cobbled courtyard below, they couldn't know.

Then an arm came from behind and grabbed the madman by the throat.

CHAPTER THREE

The Madman

"Come on, Honey," said James. "Mrs. Jarko will have to wait."

He slammed through the gate, sped over the cobblestones of the manor's inner yard, and banged unceremoniously on the iron-studded front door.

"Let me," said Honey. She took a small pick out of her pocket and did something to the lock. The door fell open.

"Brilliant," said James, wasting a moment in admiration. "They'll take you away from me someday, but brilliant."

James wasted no more moments. Up the broad oaken staircase he went, taking the steps three at a time. Then he ran down the upstairs hall with Honey close behind him.

Suddenly a stout, pleasantly smiling

woman emerged from one of the upper hall rooms.

"Someone's being attacked in that room at the end of the hall," said James. "Let me by, quickly, please."

"I'm afraid I can't permit you to enter that room," said the woman. James recognized the voice at once as that of Mrs. Evans. She sounded kind, but firm. Her English accent seemed to give her words added authority.

"But you don't understand," Honey said. "We saw someone being attacked. We think it may have been Mr. Parker. Please let us just see if he's all right. At least let James go. I'll stay here, if you like. We'll talk, you and I . . ."

James, aware that Honey was babbling merely to distract Mrs. Evans, took instant advantage of the housekeeper's shift in attention. He was down the hall in a flash. In another flash, he had shouldered in the door of what turned out indeed to be Stan Parker's private rooms.

James raced through the sitting room and into the bedroom beyond. An odd, gaunt man gave James a quick look, touched his cap, turned nervously to the casement window, and slipped out of the room.

Near the window stood the man James took to be the madman of Cornwall Crag himself, Mr. Stanley Parker, late of the Vietnam War and an assortment of mental institutions.

He stood still, running a hand through wildly disheveled hair. He was tall and slender, yet powerfully built. His great leonine head was turned away from James, gazing up into the night sky.

"Good evening, sir," James said quietly.

The handsome face turned. The dark hazel eyes were intelligent and brooding above the strong cheekbones and jaw. He looked young for his thirty-odd years, yet his face bore traces of deep suffering and great pain.

"Good evening, young man," said Stan Parker.

"Budd, James Budd," said James, coming forward and holding out his hand.

Stan Parker took it.

"Good evening, James, then. I'm Stan Parker—not that the fact can have escaped you." The voice was deep, resonant, kind, and very, very weary.

"Are you all right, sir?" James asked. He could see faint red marks at Stan's throat, as if whoever he had just been struggling with had had to nearly choke him to restrain him from—what?

"I'm all right," said Stan. "Thanks."

"You weren't in danger, then?" James asked, beginning to understand.

Stan Parker slowly shook his head. "No, James," he said. "It wasn't . . . I . . . who was in danger."

"You weren't going to jump, either?" James asked.

"Mr. Painter, my gardener, chauffeur, valet, and whatever else, numbers among his duties a sort of bodyguard service to me," said Stan. "With the help of Mrs. Evans, he keeps me from several forms of destruction, both to myself and others."

"But tonight?" James asked. "Which was it tonight? Why did Mr. Painter have to nearly choke you tonight?"

Stan Parker rubbed his forehead with a slender hand. His eyes clouded over with momentary confusion.

"To tell you the truth, James," came the deep, slow voice, "I don't know. I don't always remember. I often have to count on others to tell me."

At that moment, Mrs. Evans burst into the room.

"I don't know how to apologize for the intrusion of these young people," said Mrs. Evans. "I had asked Mr. James Budd of the Star Agency to come and help us, but I hadn't thought that he would burst in upon you in this way, sir."

"It's all right, all right," said Stan Parker.

But he turned his eyes back to the night, as if he were infinitely weary, anxious only to be let alone.

"I apologize as well," said James, charmingly and politely enough to assuage Mrs. Evans's anger. "I'm only glad to see you're all right, sir."

"Of course he's all right. How else should Mr. Parker be, with all the care we give him?" said Mrs. Evans.

She bustled about the bedroom, turning down the bed, drawing closed the vast draperies, and lighting a faint lamp by the bed.

"I'll have Mr. Painter bring you a tray of supper, Mr. Parker," she said. "Now you just settle into bed while I take these two young

people down into the kitchen for some supper and talk. We need help against those recent accusations, sir, we do. And we'll get it
all straightened out, never fear. Mr. Sam Star
will be home at the end of the week, you say,
Mr. Budd?"

James and Honey followed the chatty, bus-
tling woman down the back stairwell into a
large, shadowy kitchen. Mr. Painter left as
they came in, silently carrying a supper tray.

As Mrs. Evans began putting plates on the
kitchen table and getting things from the re-
frigerator, the back door opened as if blown
by the wind.

And through the door, also as if blown by
the wind, came the body of a beautiful, dark-
haired girl.

CHAPTER FOUR

The Madman
Disappears

"Elizabeth!" cried Mrs. Evans.
Her face went pale as she dropped to her knees beside the fallen body. She looked up at James and, in a terrified whisper, said, "It's Elizabeth. My daughter, Elizabeth."

The girl moaned and held a hand to the side of her head. James, trained by Sam and the Kings Rock medical examiner to do forensic medical examinations, knelt and gave her a quick, skilled touch.

"Nothing broken," he said. "She seems to be all right, if there's no dizziness or nausea."

"What happened?" Mrs. Evans asked, holding her daughter's hand as James and Honey helped the girl to a chair.

"I don't know, mother," the pretty girl said. "I'd been out riding, and I wanted a walk to stretch my legs. I was coming across the

35

fields when someone suddenly came up behind me. I wasn't hit. I just felt something
like a pinch, here"—she rubbed a place behind her ear— "and I was out like a light. I
don't even know how long I was unconscious
before I managed to stagger back here."

"Who could have done such a horrid thing
to you, Liz?" Mrs. Evans asked, growing
more and more agitated.

"Had to be someone with medical knowl-
edge," said James, "or at least some knowl-
edge of the nervous system. Not many people would know enough about pressure
points to make someone black out."

Mrs. Evans wrung her hands and said
something. Her English accent seemed to
become more pronounced as she grew more
upset, and James had trouble understanding
her.

"What mother is saying," said Liz, "is that
Mr. Parker spent some time as a paramedic
when he was in the navy."

"I see," said James.

"And what's that you said about the full
moon?" Honey asked Mrs. Evans.

"It's around the time of the full moon that
Mr. Parker's . . . spells . . . are at their worst,"

said Mrs. Evans clearly enough for all of them to understand.

"And it's near the time of the full moon now, you mean," said James. "So what you're suggesting, Mrs. Evans, is that Mr. Parker may have had something to do with what happened to Liz."

Mrs. Evans nodded. But she quickly added, as she put the kettle on for tea, "Our fault—Mr. Painter's and mine. We're hired to protect him from himself. Our fault, Mr. Budd, Miss Mack. He can't always help himself when the fit is upon him."

James paused a moment before he asked the next question.

"It was my impression, Mrs. Evans, that you called the Star Agency on behalf of Mr. Parker, that you believed he wasn't to blame for the grave robberies, for the other things he's suspected of doing. Are you now saying that, due to these 'spells,' as you call them, Mr. Parker may be guilty after all?"

"Mr. Parker isn't responsible," said Mrs. Evans. "That's what I'm saying. Please help him, Mr. Budd. Please help him."

James's eyes flickered in a way only Honey understood. "Our fee is three hundred dollars a day, plus expenses," he said. Mrs. Evans nodded her acceptance.

Before Honey and James left, James turned to the pretty, dark-haired Liz. Her brown eyes flashed at James, and her slim, curving figure moved provocatively about the kitchen as if she hadn't just been unconscious at all.

"Will you be all right?" asked James.

"Will you be back?" asked Liz.

"Of course we will," said Honey sweetly, deftly coming between James and the girl with a look that said, *We'll protect you with everything we've got, but your hand will come off at the wrist if you touch him.*

"That's my girl," said James, enjoying the display hugely, and sweeping Honey out of the kitchen, back through the great hall, and out the front door to the waiting Firebird.

"Why haven't we seen Liz Evans before?" asked Honey as they drove back toward Kings Rock.

"We'll head for Charlie and his computer," said James. "He'll track down school and police records and see if we can find anything on her."

"You didn't buy something back there,

James," said Honey. "I saw that flicker in your eye."

"It may be my naturally suspicious nature," said James. "But I'm not as sure now as I was when we got there of how helpful Mrs. Evans has really been to Mr. Parker. There's something about her that doesn't quite wash."

"I wonder," said Honey thoughtfully.

"There's something else here that doesn't wash," James said suddenly. "I can't brake, and we're already going over ninety."

They were still coming down out of the bluffs and not yet near the flat of the prairie.

"There isn't much we can run into," said James, as he kept trying the brake pedal and the emergency brake handle.

"All we'd need is a bump or a rock in the road, and we could roll over—trip over our own wheels, so to speak," said Honey, only half joking. "We're doing a hundred and ten now," she added, looking over at the speedometer.

"Blast," said James. "*Blast!*" he swore again at the top of his lungs, as he tried once more and failed to slow the Firebird down.

Suddenly the headlights went out.

"That does it," said James. "This is no accidental failure. A braking problem, maybe. A total engine failure, maybe. But just brakes and headlights—that's no accidental problem, that's attempted murder!"

"Who?" Honey yelled over the sound of the speeding engine.

"Who later," James yelled back. "What—as in 'What do we do?'—is more important right now."

The Firebird careened faster and faster down Rock Bluffs toward Old Cattle Road. James hoped to heaven no one was on it. Expertly, he headed the car down the hilly road and zoomed onto the road leading to Kings Rock.

"Didn't Charlie provide for an emergency like this?" Honey shouted.

"I've got automatic electronics for opening both ends of the garage," James shouted back, "oil slicks and smoke-screen emissions at the touch of a button, and an assortment of beepers and call systems in this car. But extra brakes?"

"Here!" Honey cried out. "James, here they are! There's a foot pedal under the center of the dashboard. Try it."

Charlie had done it again. He had obviously doubled the equipment of the braking system, and put in an extra brake pedal.

"I wish Charlie had remembered to tell me about that," said James, as he slowed down at last. But the relief in his voice was clear. A powerful flashlight he kept in the glove compartment lit them down Old Cattle Road.

James and Honey recovered from danger as quickly as they often got into it. Seconds later, they had settled down again.

"Do you think Stan Parker had anything to do with what happened to the car just now?" Honey asked.

"No," said James, rolling down High Street now.

Charlie Alda lived just a few doors from the Star Agency. James parked the Firebird in the alleyway behind High Street and led the way through Mrs. Alda's hydrangea bushes into the Alda back yard.

It was getting late, but Charlie was still up, out back in his shed.

As they crossed the yard, Honey said, "You liked Stan Parker, didn't you, James?"

James nodded. "Instantly."

The lights in the shed were on full blaze.

Charlie's father, supportive of Charlie's scientific genius, and a builder in his own right, had built the shed for Charlie to use as a lab and as a private retreat from his five younger brothers and sisters.

"You can understand my gloom about the overcrowded conditions on this planet," Charlie often said. "My own personal experience makes me want to make *any* contribution I can to *any* technology program willing to help me resettle on *any* other planet."

The shed, as James and Honey entered, was filled not only with the usual Bunsen burners, tubes, and flasks, but also high-tech models of satellites, space stations, and rockets, and, on the table near the door, Charlie's pride and joy. In return for working after school at Torello's Hardware Store, Mr. Torello had sold Charlie his used Apple II computer for a reasonable price. Included with the 64K computer, keyboard, and display monitor, were two disc drives, a printer, and a modem. Charlie was saving for a laboratory data analyzer.

"Can you log into all the schools, hospitals, and police blotters around here?" James asked Charlie.

"Do you mean in the next five minutes?" Charlie asked blandly, his owlish eyes large behind his glasses and under his mop of curly blond hair. "Or have I got an hour?"

James's favorite part of the Apple II was the modem and its CompuServe connection. With CompuServe, Charlie could do everything from tracking the stock market to getting news off the Associated Press wire. He used it mostly for electronic mail—it gave him access to everyone else on the service and all their information. James especially liked being able to use Charlie's computer buddies and their terminals to make any long-distance telephone connection they wanted.

"All ready," said Charlie. He punched a few keys, picked up the modem, and spoke into it.

On the screen appeared student lists from all the towns nearest Kings Rock: Madison to the north, Loup Falls to the east, Arcadia to the south, and Spalding to the west.

"There, Spalding, same grade as ours," said James.

ELIZABETH (LIZ) EVANS had appeared on the screen right away.

"So," said James, "for whatever reason, she doesn't go to our school, which is nearest, but to Spalding High School."

"Look again," said Honey.

ELIZABETH (LIZ) EVANS had appeared on the screen once more. This time it was a police listing for shoplifting.

"Maybe her shoplifting is a habit her mother doesn't want known in her home town," said Charlie.

"Possibly," said James. "Possibly. There may be something else, too, something about both of them that Mrs. Evans doesn't want known." He filled Charlie in on the madman of Cornwall Crag—the little he knew of the circumstances, the local accusations that Stan Parker was responsible for the grave robberies and the theft of Mrs. Jarko's rabbits, the new suspicion that he had something to do with knocking Liz Evans unconscious.

Just then the telephone rang—Charlie had his own line in the shed, connected to the phones in the Alda house.

"For you," said Charlie. "Chief Adams."

James just listened as the chief spoke. Then he said, "Yes," and hung up.

"Mrs. Evans just called the chief," he told Honey and Charlie. "Stan Parker is gone, missing from Cornwall Crag. Tomorrow night is the height of the full moon, the time when Mr. Parker is most dangerous. Chief Adams has issued an APB. He's sent out three cars tonight, called for a helicopter for tomorrow, and is on his way to Cornwall Crag himself. He wants to know if we'll give him a hand after school tomorrow."

"Why the panic?" asked Charlie.

"Two barns and a silo across the fields toward Madison have been set on fire," said James quietly. "The animals were let out in time, and no one's been hurt—yet."

"People are blaming Mr. Parker?" Honey asked.

James nodded. "People are blaming Mr. Parker," he said.

CHAPTER FIVE

Hands Dripping Blood

"Charlie," said James, "can you rig some kind of beeper transmitter for me?"

"Sure," said Charlie agreeably. "Why not?"

"When we find Stan Parker, I'd like to keep track of him for a while. Also, Charlie, could you get everybody set up for tomorrow?"

"Sure," said Charlie agreeably. "Why not?"

The following afternoon after school, their closest friends appeared at the kung fu practice hall on the Kawabata farm.

The Kawabata family had come from Japan to live among the cornfields of Nebraska. They had brought with them Zen Buddhism, with its meditation, its attention to the beautiful details of life, its painting, tea ceremony, archery, and the practice of judo, kung fu, and karate. On their farm on Old Cattle Road, where they grew feed crops and raised dairy cows, the barns and silos were bright red American buildings, but their home, their meditation and practice halls, their teahouse and rock gardens were Japanese. James and his friends came here often, to meditate, and to learn from Mr. Kawabata how to act from love rather than anger, even in a violent world.

The friends were there that Tuesday afternoon, ready to help in any way they could. They gathered around James and Honey in their white kimono jackets and practice trousers.

When James finished talking to them, finished describing the horrors of empty graves and burning barns, and explaining the connection between Stan Parker's illness and the full moon, his voice grew quiet.

"I'm not convinced of Mr. Parker's guilt," he said. "I am convinced a man has a right to be free until or unless his actions prove otherwise. Will you help?"

Honey already stood beside James. Charlie, who was devoted to James, volunteered first.

"With you," said Tad Kawabata, who assisted his father in teaching them martial arts.

"If Honey's involved, you can count on me," said a tall, beautiful black girl named Kathy Howard. Honey's closest friend besides James, Kathy had three passions in life: being gorgeous, falling in love often, and astrophysics. Kathy's idea of heaven was to be up in a NASA Spacelab, along with five men, wearing something chic in a spacesuit.

"Me, too," said Clara Rand, Kings Rock High School's best artist. "I don't need to start painting the decorations for the Rock for a couple of weeks, so I've got plenty of time." The Rock was the senior high school dance held every year at the end of October.

Joe Levy, their star football player, and Jilly Bruce, their best actress and president of the Drama Club, were the next to volunteer. "With his muscle and my timing, we're a natural pair of hunters," said Jilly.

"Thanks, all of you," said James, after all the people in the practice hall had volunteered with their usual good humor and friendship and spirit.

There was a sudden noise behind one of

the rice-paper screens. Joe Levy looked behind the screen, and with one hand pulled out a skinny, leather-jacketed, mean-faced, narrow-eyed person.

"Look what I've got," said Joe, making a face as if he'd eaten something sour.

"Trouble," said James, not quite laughing.

Trouble for James often came in the form of Ratso Jones and his two sidekicks, Tom and Sharky. The Rat Gang's mission in life was to trip up James Budd wherever possible. They operated out of an old abandoned shack not far from the railroad station, where Ratso's father was stationmaster. Ratso used the shack not only as a clubhouse, but for making deals, storing stolen goods, and for occasional beatings. James had seen enough police and medical reports on Ratso's victims to be thoroughly disgusted by Ratso Jones.

"Shall I break him in half and just get it over with?" Tad offered.

"If anyone gets him, I do." Honey Mack's sweet voice rang across the hall. Honey got nervous when James was threatened, and she often protected him faster than he needed protection—sometimes even when he didn't need it at all. Ratso watched her now as she advanced menacingly, flicking her long, golden mane, ready to throw a double sunfist punch that could disable a rhinoceros.

"I'll go, I'll go," Ratso yelled.

"Don't come back—ever," shouted Kathy, Joe, and a few others.

"He will," James said calmly. "He always does."

Impeccable in his practice clothes, James sat down in a perfect lotus position on a black *zazan* cushion to go over the details of the search he was planning.

"We'll divide into four groups, the way Chief Adams has deployed his own men," he began. "Joe and Jilly, you each head a group. Tad, you head the third, and I'll take Honey, Kathy, and Charlie with me."

After a brief discussion about times and meeting places, James said quietly, "My group will take horses from the farm, Tad, if your father will let us. I want to go places we can't reach by car. Honey and Kathy and I will ride out, and we'll bring a horse for Charlie. Charlie, can you drive the Firebird out to Cornwall Crag? We may need it later."

"Sure," said Charlie, taking the keys from James. Tad went to get the horses ready.

"We may be out all night," James went on. "Everybody dress warmly and bring canteens and whatever else you think you might need. I don't have to remind you, no weapons."

Sam Star, whom James adored unconditionally, was the smartest man James had ever met. He had the only opinions James cared about besides his own. Sam didn't hit. He didn't like guns. And he had brought James up the same way.

"I also want to remind us all," said James, "that no matter what you hear, people are innocent until proven otherwise. Clear?"

"Don't worry, James," said Clara. "We've got the message that you don't believe the gossip about the madman of Cornwall Crag. We'll remember."

"Thanks," said James. "Thanks to you all."

It was five o'clock when James, Honey, and Kathy—leading a stallion for Charlie—mounted their horses at the Kawabata farm to ride north into the fields, crags, and pitted prairie land that made up the Cornwall Estate. No one had cared for the land for years, and it had become a wilderness dangerous to anyone not familiar with it. They met Charlie coming across a barren field from Cornwall Crag.

"We have only a few hours of daylight," said James. "The police have been searching all day without sighting Mr. Parker. It's up to us now."

James handed them each a powerful flashlight to attach to their saddles. "And," said James, "we have Band-Aid."

Band-Aid was a black Labrador retriever who lived next door to the Star Agency but ate with, slept with, and generally hung out with James. The special training James had given Band-Aid—not to mention the dog's affectionate loyalty—was often a great help in James's cases.

Accompanied by the black dog, the four rode off into the darkening afternoon.

Over the next few hours, they separated, came together, got cold and hungry, and by turns grew hopeful and then despairing about finding Stan Parker. Into the night they rode—through open places where it was fine underfoot; through bracken where the horses stumbled among pitted bogs; through the darkness of trees and bramble.

James had ridden off a way by himself, over a crest and beyond a copse of trees. It was growing late, and he was wondering whether they ought to give it up for the night. He was wondering whether they should have begun not by looking for the man, but by searching for the contents of the coffins, or for clues among the cinders of the barns and silo.

Suddenly, ahead of James, high on the crag above, outlined against the fullest, whitest moon James had ever seen, was the wildly gesturing figure of a man.

James urged his black stallion into a gallop, hoping to reach the man before he could escape.

But the man never moved. All he did was hold out his hands to James in despair. The hands, James could see in the moonlight, were dripping with blood.

CHAPTER SIX

Stan Parker's Secret

James galloped his black stallion up the rocky crag. Band-Aid was beside him, barking at James's sudden movements, at the slowly rising full moon, at the strangeness and terror of the blood-stained figure on the crest above.

"Don't move," James called.

"Where would I go?" came the reply, in the same deep, resonant, weary tone James had heard for the first time the night before.

As James drew near, his horse reared at the sudden smell of blood. James leaped down, and as he approached the man, he saw that every part of Stan Parker seemed wracked with pain—not physical pain, but mental anguish. And once again, blood or no blood, reputation notwithstanding, James felt a rush of sympathy for someone misunderstood.

Yet the master of Cornwall Crag stood

there, against the silver of the full moon, covered in blood, staring down in horror at a small coyote that lay bleeding at his feet.

James bent to look at the animal. He touched it gently, examining its wound. Then he took off his navy nylon jacket and wrapped the small coyote in it.

"My horse will carry us both," said James softly to the tormented man. "Mr. Parker, will you come?"

The dark hazel eyes looked up at the young detective, who was now astride the stallion. With one hand James held the small wounded animal on his lap; with the other he reached out to Stan Parker.

The man gave a short laugh, ran a hand through his wild hair, and with a practiced leap mounted the horse behind James. James cantered the animal back toward the gray, forbidding stone manor house of Cornwall Crag.

The rest of the search party hadn't yet returned. It was just as well. James wanted a few moments alone with Stan Parker.

In the kitchen, James laid the coyote on the table. The animal looked frightened, but it never whimpered.

"Brave little thing," said James. He

washed the blood from the animal's wounded leg, found a piece of straight, strong wood from the fireplace, and made a splint, which he bound to the leg with a clean dish towel. Then he made a pillowed nest near the fire, set down a bowl of milk, and left the animal there to sleep and recover.

That done, James turned to Stan Parker, who had washed what blood he could from his hands and removed his blood-stained sweater.

"The animal seems to be all right," Stan said. "Perhaps the attack is over for this month—at least, I hope it is. Blast that Gary Painter, and Mrs. Evans, too. They're supposed to keep me in restraints during the few days of the full moon. They know my horrible, dark secrets." The bitter sarcasm in his voice was directed at himself.

"Mr. Parker," James said, "I know nothing of your horrible, dark secrets. I hope you will tell me. But for now, rest assured, you've done absolutely nothing wrong. That coyote's leg was caught in a steel-jaw trap. The animal broke its leg trying to free itself. I believe you were trying to help it. You most certainly didn't hurt it. Is your mind often in confusion like this?"

The tall, powerful man flung himself into a chair in front of the fire. The deep stone fireplace was a roaring cavern half as big as the huge kitchen itself, with a chimney large enough to catch the rushing prairie winds.

"Will you talk to me?" James asked. His voice had a kindness to which Stan Parker responded. He began:

"I was still in my teens when I was sent to Vietnam. I won't defend the stupidity with which I bought the nonsense all nations tell their young to convince them to go kill people and be killed. My God, James, all divisions between people and nations are the cause of war, and so stupid. Anyway, at eighteen, I bought the whole thing. I was in the navy, in the jungle, in the Mekong Delta. The first thing I discovered was that the people they called my enemies were just as young, just as scared as I was."

James leaned against the mantel, arms folded, eyes fixed on the suffering man.

Stan Parker went on. "I was a petty officer, second class. Part of my job was to train South Vietnamese farm boys, who knew nothing of machines, how to handle modern weapons. We taught them everything from how to han-

dle rifles and small arms to demolition and
guerrilla tactics. We taught them how to carry
out raids against transportation and commu-
nications systems. They thought it was a lark
at first, ambushing supply convoys. At first I
thought it was a lark, too. There wasn't much
loss of life then, and none of it was up close.
Also, I still believed that war might be
hell, but some of it had a point. What an idiot
I was! Imagine, taking young boys who
grew food in the sunlight of the fields, and
teaching them to kill—and calling it hero-
ism! I helped turn healthy children into
slaughterers!"

Stan Parker rested his head in his hands.

"Then began the worst. I was ordered to
lead the Vietnamese boys and our own men
on some search-and-destroy missions. You
cannot imagine the horror of those, James.
You're told every man, woman, and child is a
potential enemy. You go on patrol, you see
someone, you give an order, and those unsea-
soned child-soldiers, scared to death and often high on drugs, go berserk. There is a
sense of power so horrible it's beyond explaining. You kill anything. It's nothing like
the movies or television. It's a nightmare you

can't imagine. Once it starts, no one can stop it. To stop it you'd have to shoot your own men. And even then it wouldn't stop, because anyone who tried to stop the killing would himself be killed."

James, riveted by what he was hearing, sat down in the chair on the other side of the fireplace.

"You know, back home people thought only the unbalanced men behaved like that," said Stan Parker, shaking his head. "Don't think it! We're all capable of going berserk from fear in the middle of a jungle full of gunfire. Especially a kid just eighteen, twenty years old, away from home and terrified and high from gun power.

"Anyway, it broke me. It wasn't the fear that got me, or the fear that I, too, was going mad with power. It was the shock that I had bought the whole, dumb thing about its being okay to kill *anyone*. I couldn't bear that I had ever believed it was all right to take life, that I had even taught others to do so. So," ended Stan, "I cracked."

"And then?" prompted James.

"Then, after my discharge, came the mental institutions. There were several. The last one was in England, a sanitarium out on the Yorkshire moors. Mrs. Evans was a nurse there. When I decided to leave and come home, to live out my days in solitude here at Cornwall Crag, I knew I would need a pair of strong keepers. You see, James, while for most of the month I'm as calm as a spring breeze—I play my music, write my novels, grow my roses—for about a week, around the full moon, I'm mad as a March hare. Whatever happened to me during the war twisted itself into that strange form when I was in England and has stayed with me ever since. During those six days or so, I am apparently capable of great violence. I rob graves or burn barns or maim small creatures. It's all too ghastly to believe."

"So you brought Mrs. Evans and Mr. Painter from England to act as your keepers?" said James. "And what do you mean by 'apparently'?"

"Only that afterwards, I don't remember my spells or fits or whatever they are, or what I do during those periods," said Stan. "Mrs. Evans generally tells me, especially if it's something awful."

"And Liz?" said James.

"Liz is Mrs. Evans's daughter," said Stan. "I know little about her, except that I believe she has a tendency to cause her mother trouble from time to time."

"Do you remember knocking Liz unconscious last night?" James asked, purposely blunt.

Stan Parker raised dark, gleaming eyes.

"Dear God," he whispered, and stalked from the room.

One of their rules as detectives, Honey knew, was never to do anything before checking with your partner. But Honey also knew, as she peered into the kitchen, that James was having a serious discussion with Stan Parker. Politely, she left, and wandered out into the hall again.

As she passed a hanging tapestry, Honey heard voices in conversation. Impolitely this time, she listened.

"What've you got for me tonight, Liz?" said a voice Honey knew well—well enough to detest.

"These, Ratso," said the sultry voice of Liz Evans. Honey could picture the pretty girl with the long, dark curls and the dark, teasing eyes.

"Where'd you get them?" Ratso asked.

Honey moved closer to the tapestry. There might have been an open door behind the wall hanging, or perhaps there was just an opening in the wall. Whatever, Honey could hear the two as if she were in the same room with them. Trying hard to breathe quietly, she leaned in closer.

"The shopping mall outside Arcadia," Liz was saying. "It's a real easy place to pick stuff up. There are so many boutiques, you can be in and out of a whole row of them before anyone sees you have anything in your pockets at all. This stuff any good to you?"

"Everything you deliver is good to me," said Ratso. "Sold the bracelets and earrings for twice what they were worth. Sold the cameras for three times. The watches you lifted from that place in Loup Falls went over great, too."

"What about these silver rings and chains?" Liz asked anxiously.

"Gold would have been better, but these'll do," Ratso replied. "Silver's harder to get rid of, so it'll take me a little longer to fence this."

"Hey," protested Liz. "It's just as hard to lift silver as gold. Why should I suffer?"

"We'll both suffer, if you don't shut up," said Ratso in a threatening tone.

Honey heard a scuffle. Thinking Ratso had made a nasty dive for Liz, she was about to go for help when suddenly she herself was yanked into the inner room.

"What the—?" Liz began.

"Well, if it isn't James Budd's busybody girlfriend," said Ratso. "She's got her nose in everybody's business almost as much as he does. Pain in the neck, with her fast motorcycle and her fast mouth."

He had a painful grip on Honey's arm, twisting it behind her back. He gave it an extra twist, and the pain brought tears to Honey's eyes. But she didn't make a sound. Playing around with Ratso was serious. And Honey was as concerned for Liz as she was for her own safety.

"Liz, you shouldn't be messing around with him," she said. "He's a pretty nasty piece of business. I mean, if you get in his way, he'd think nothing of wrecking your face, your head . . ."

This time the twist was worse. Honey screamed.

Liz's eyes clouded with fear. She fled— warned, Honey hoped, against Ratso Jones for good.

But now, with his newest working shoplifter gone because of her, Ratso was angrier than ever at Honey. Honey knew he wouldn't hesitate to break both her arms. She also knew that Liz was too frightened to bring help. Honey was alone, and in pain, and too far away from James now to yell for help.

CHAPTER SEVEN

Liz's Secret

As Stan Parker left the firelit kitchen, Honey Mack dashed in.

"You found him," she said. "I'm glad Mr. Parker was here. Good for you, James."

She told James briefly what had happened behind the tapestry, and once again they were both grateful to Mr. Kawabata and his lessons in self-defense.

"I got one hand loose and used the coiling snake technique," said Honey. "Ratso won't use his arms again too comfortably for a couple of days."

She went to the fire for a moment's warmth and dropped to her knees next to the coyote, which stared up at her with large, frightened eyes.

"Oh, my dear," said Honey softly. "Where did you come from?" She touched the small head, and the creature instantly relaxed and closed its eyes again.

James smiled at Honey. All living things—himself included—seemed to feel more secure at her touch. She came over for a kiss, and James held her close for a minute or two.

"I'll tell you about the coyote—and Mr. Parker—soon," he said as they broke from their hug. "But first we'd better tell the others they can stop searching."

"Kathy and Charlie are waiting just outside," said Honey. "The three of us will scatter and tell the other groups they can go home. I'll be back in a while. Yes?"

"Yes," said James. "In the meantime, I'll call Sam. There are a few things I want to check out with him. Then we'll talk to Mrs. Evans, Mr. Painter, and Liz. There are some questions we need to ask them."

Honey went off, and James found a telephone in the upstairs library. He dialed the special number in Europe that Sam had given him. Sam was on the line in minutes.

"He can't have done all that stuff, Sam," James said. "I've talked to him. He's been to hell and back, seen violence for what it is." James described everything that had hap-

pened, repeated all he'd been told by Chief
Adams, by Mrs. Evans, by Stan Parker himself. "I just don't buy it," James went on. "For
one thing, Stan Parker is taller and thinner
than the person I saw escaping from the
graveyard. For another, he'd have had to
make a really hard run to be in the right place
to attack Liz Evans. And he just doesn't have
the temperament for assaulting rabbits and
coyotes— or anyone or anything at all."

"You don't buy it? Don't buy it," said Sam,
who always spoke into telephones as if he
were sending telegrams. "You don't think
Stan Parker's capable of that stuff? Don't
think it."

"Thanks," said James, grateful at how completely Sam trusted his judgment.

"What're you going to work on next?" Sam
asked.

"I want to check out the creepy figure in
the graveyard, and find those bodies from the
empty coffins. The other questions are obvi-
ous. Who hurt Liz? Who set the barns on fire?
Who set the coyote trap? I know Mr. Parker
was trying to help that animal, not hurt it,
Sam. And I'm just as certain he had nothing
to do with the other stuff. Someone's con-

vinced Mr. Parker he's a madman, and convinced the rest of the world as well. Mr. Parker may believe it. Kings Rock may believe it. I don't," said James with absolute conviction.

"Then find out who the real madman is," said Sam. "Find out soon. Sounds as if the crimes are coming closer together. Find out why."

"Right," said James.

"Love to Honey," said Sam.

"Right," said James, and rang off.

As he put down the receiver, Liz Evans walked into the library. As James watched her move, he realized that the word "walked" didn't quite describe the way the small, curvaceous girl, with the mass of dark, curly hair and the dark, seductive eyes, crossed the room. Her movements were like a slow, wonderful dance no man could take his eyes from.

"Good," said James aloud, steadying himself with the sound of his own voice. "I've got some questions to ask you."

"Anything," said Liz. Under her lowered lashes, her dark eyes flashed.

"Sit there," said James, leaning against the

desk and pointing to a chair a few feet away.

"Anything," said Liz again, looking up at James in her smoldering way.

"My first question is, why don't we all know you?" said James. "You live near Kings Rock. Why don't you go to our school?"

"I steal," said Liz. "I've been kicked out of a lot of schools around here. They don't seem to like thieves."

Liz spoke as if there weren't much difference between being a thief and being a cheerleader. Stealing was just what she happened to do, instead of, say, playing basketball.

"Mother says it's my vagabond blood," said Liz. "My father was an itinerant actor traveling across England when my mother met him." Liz shrugged. "Whatever the reason, I've never understood people who don't take what they want. I don't take anything from anyone who's poor. But a dress in a store? If I want it, I take it. If someone leaves a locker open and I see something I like, I take it."

Liz rose and moved silkily toward James, her eyes suggesting that she had once again found something she wanted.

"Poor Liz, how is your head this evening?"

came a velvety voice from the doorway.

Honey had always moved faster than anyone else in Kings Rock. In a flash she was across the room and between Liz and James.

"Not that I blame you, child," said Honey. "He's absolutely divine. But he's mine, you know, so mustn't touch. Who knocked you out, do you think?" Honey's tone altered entirely as she touched Liz's head to feel whether the lump on her scalp had subsided.

"I don't have to think who got me," said Liz. "It's Stan Parker who got me. He's the madman, you know. It's no use investigating, or whatever you call it. He's the crazy one around here."

With those words, Liz flounced from the room. Whether she was angry at having been knocked out or at not getting to James, Honey wasn't sure.

"What do you think, James?" Honey asked.

"I think it gives a man an interesting feeling to have . . ."

"If you say two pretty girls fighting over him, I'll scream," said Honey.

" . . . to have his girl protect him," James said smoothly, giving Honey a kiss.

"Handsome devil," said Honey.

"Gorgeous girl," said James.

For a moment, James lost himself, his thoughts, and everything else around him in the long silence of Honey's kiss.

The ring of the telephone interrupted both the kiss and the silence. Without thinking, James picked up the receiver.

It was Mrs. Jarko. She was so upset, she didn't care who was at the other end. "A ghost!" she screeched. "Out on the prairie. She's out there walking on the prairie now. Too many doings around here these days, too many doings!"

CHAPTER EIGHT

Ghost on the Prairie

The figure of a woman in white walked under the brilliance of the full moon, solitary against the night sky. She moved slowly, ghostly and silent on the prairie. And she moved in danger, for this part of the prairie was wild, boggy marshland, almost as if it had been brought from England along with the gray stones of the manor house.

Honey, Kathy, and Charlie stood just outside the house, transfixed by the "ghost" Mrs. Jarko had spoken of.

"Isn't she lovely," Honey breathed at last.

"Look at the fall of that white cloak over the dress," said Kathy, "and those gathered sleeves. She's something out of another time and place."

"If she's real at all," said Charlie, his eyes wide behind the horn-rimmed glasses. "And

73

if she is, she almost makes it worth hanging in on this planet a little while longer."

As the three were growing rhapsodic over the beauty of the ghost, James, more interested in its substance, had crept silently across the bogs toward the woman in white. Taking her by surprise, he caught the woman's wrist. Startled, she let out a little cry and tried to pull free.

"I'm not going to hurt you," said James. "I only want to know who you are. Someone has reported a ghost. I thought I'd better come and warn you before some superstitious idiot takes it into his head to do you some harm."

The woman still struggled. James held fast and smiled down at her. She was tiny, with feathery, dark-blond hair and large, intense eyes. Those eyes were both frightened and angry, and reflected her determination to be left alone. Small though she was, she was far from fragile, and she managed to shake James loose with a twist of her arm. Panting, she stood her ground and imperiously held up her head.

"And who are you, young man?" she demanded.

James didn't know whether to bow in deference to her commanding air, or smile at her tininess. She seemed to be about the same age as Stan Parker, and therefore, James decided, merited respect. He bowed and smiled at the same time.

"James Budd," said James. "I'm James Budd, at your service, ma'am. And you? May I ask who you are?"

"If you will first tell me who or what a James Budd is," she said.

A woman of character and intelligence, James thought, *as well as great loveliness.*

Aloud, he said, "I've been asked to investigate the case of Mr. Stanley Parker of Cornwall Crag. There has been some gossip, there have been some accusations."

"And your position?" the woman asked. Her voice seemed very caring, very anxious.

James usually didn't discuss cases with strangers, but he knew instinctively that this woman could be trusted. "I like Mr. Parker," he said. "I don't think he's capable of hurting anyone or anything."

The woman in white sighed with relief.

"My name, Mr. Budd, is Dana Winter," she

said, offering a small, graceful hand in a very firm handshake. She did not seem at all ghostly—or even reserved—now.

"And who, will you please tell me, is Dana Winter?" James asked. He gave her his arm, to lead her back to the relative safety of the drier prairie land, away from the damp of the marsh. "Where do you live?"

"I've been living on the rim of things," she said, "haunting a life that isn't, yet is, my own."

By this time, Honey, Kathy, and Charlie had drawn near. James introduced them. They all circled the tiny woman—as if she were from another world and needed protection in this one, James thought.

In the moonlight, walking together across the wild moorlike prairie, they listened as Dana Winter told her lonely story.

"It isn't a long story, really," she began. "Stan and I fell in love when we were twenty, not long after he had been sent overseas. He was on leave in Japan. We met in a lovely teahouse garden, under a moon like this one."

Dana smiled at the memory. But the smile faded as she told them that shortly after they fell in love, Stan was sent back to the war. "In a way, he never came back to me," she said. "After the war there were the hospitals, the sanitariums."

Honey's comforting arm went around Dana's small shoulders. The woman's dark, intense eyes shone with gratitude. Then she pulled away, as if she might be undone by giving in to sympathy.

"I've had my work," she said. She mentioned two published novels. "And I love Stan. But he won't let me come to him. He knows that I'm always near, that I follow wherever he goes. But he's afraid he'll hurt me, you see. He's shut himself away from the world, from living any kind of normal life, from being with people, even from me. He thinks he doesn't deserve to live." Dana Winter shuddered. "And yet he cannot die. It's so awful for him."

"For you, too," said Kathy.

Charlie Alda stared wide-eyed at the beautiful woman, as if he were star-struck. Dana Winter smiled at him, James noticed approvingly. He liked people who were aware of other people, even through their own pain.

"We're going to help you, Miss Winter," said James. "You and Mr. Parker. It's going to be all right."

"Let's go to the manor now," said Honey. "All of us."

"Oh, no!" cried the woman. "No!" And before any of them could stop her, before they could find out why the suggestion upset her so, she fled into the rising mists. So swiftly did she go that even James could not follow her.

CHAPTER NINE

Danger in the Mists

Back at Cornwall Crag, James rushed upstairs to the telephone in the library.

"Chief Adams, please," James said, and held as the desk sergeant at the police station put him through.

"Chief Adams speaking," came the voice of the burly police chief of Kings Rock.

James relayed all the evening's information, straight through the sudden flight of Dana Winter.

"Must be something wrong with the guy if even his ladylove is scared of him, James," said Chief Adams.

"She believes in him completely," said James. "All I suggested is that we come back to Cornwall Crag. It may be something else here, Chief—not Mr. Parker himself—that she's afraid of."

"Interesting thought," said Chief Adams. "You have any idea what?"

"I don't think it's *what*," said James. "I think it's *who*."

"You may have a point," said Chief Adams. "If what you say is true, that Stan Parker isn't a madman and hasn't committed the felonies, then someone else is doing a good job of pinning the stuff on him. Can you handle it up there? Shall I send someone?"

"Let me start," said James. "If I need help, I'll call. For now, I think I'll find out more if we do it quietly."

"Okay, I'll give you a couple of days," said Chief Adams. "But if anything else goes wrong, I'm going to have to step in. Sure you don't want me to send out a couple of patrol cars to find the woman in white?"

"You said a couple of days," said James.

"I did," said the chief. "You got them."

When James returned the receiver to its cradle and turned around, Mrs. Evans was in the doorway. How long had she been standing there, James wondered; how much more did she know?

The woman smiled a bright, good-natured smile. "How about some coffee, some late supper, Mr. Budd?" she asked in a kind, cheerful voice. "You all must be exhausted from the search this evening, and from the sad business over Mr. Parker. I feel so sorry that Mr. Painter and I lost him. I can't think how he got out of his room to roam the prairie and hurt that poor little coyote."

As James followed the housekeeper down the stairs to the vast kitchen, he listened to her chatter on about the evening's events, clucking over everything as if it were all routine in caring for the master of the house.

"Sometimes it's all I can do, looking after that wayward child of mine and poor Mr. Parker, to say nothing of making sure that old lazybones Gary Painter takes care of the gardens and the cars," Mrs. Evans went on.

In the kitchen, Kathy, Charlie, and Honey were waiting for James. They were all eager to go home and get a few hours' sleep before school. Almost before they knew it, though, Mrs. Evans had put scrambled eggs, toast, and orange juice on the table, and a pot of coffee on the stove.

"Charlie," said James evenly, "you have the Firebird around here somewhere, don't you?"

"Yes," said Charlie.

"And in the Firebird is that little number of yours, isn't it?" asked James.

"Yes," said Charlie. He knew perfectly well that James meant the beeper transmitter he had rigged up.

As Mrs. Evans finished pouring the coffee and went upstairs, James dashed outside for a couple of minutes. He was back in time to see Mrs. Evans come downstairs wearing a coat as if she were going out in the chilly autumn night.

"I have to pay a neighbor a small visit," she said sweetly. "She's feeling poorly, and I promised to bring her a little something. I'll be back soon. Enjoy your eggs and toast now."

As soon as she was gone, James said, "I think we'll soon know something more about what's going on around here. I think wherever Mrs. Evans is going at two o'clock in the morning will tell us a great deal. Eat quickly, everyone. You could take a little time now, couldn't you, to look around Cornwall Crag—say, for the contents of the emptied coffins?"

"What about you?" asked Honey.

"I'll be in the Firebird, tracking Mrs. Evans. As soon as I find out where she's headed, I'll be back."

As he drove out across the dirt road, at a safe distance behind Mrs. Evans's car, James wished that he had checked Stan Parker's room before he'd left. He had just sent his three best friends down into the depths and dungeons of the old stone house to search for the bones of the dead, and he hadn't made certain of the whereabouts of Mr. Parker. He didn't know where Dana Winter had gotten to. And he had only two days to put all the pieces together before Chief Adams sent in the troops.

"All right, then," James muttered to the night. "Two days it is."

He geared down the Firebird until it hummed as quietly as possible through the swirling mists. In the rear-view mirror, James could see the manor's towers and turrets reflecting moonlight through the fog. A light shone from a single casement. Stan Parker's rooms?

James drove on through the luminous mists, which now completely enshrouded the manor from view. The wind was rushing across the prairie, and James wondered if he was following Mrs. Evans into a rising tempest. He could see only a few feet ahead of him. Only Charlie's transmitter told James where Mrs. Evans was now.

The beeper was suddenly quiet. James couldn't see, but he could hear Mrs. Evans's car stop. He stopped the Firebird and went the rest of the way on foot.

About a hundred feet down the road, there was a small outbuilding. Creeping around to a back window, James peered inside. Yellow light from a naked bulb illuminated the figure of a man, whom James immediately recognized as Gary Painter. He was clearly waiting for Mrs. Evans. They began to talk the minute Mrs. Evans entered the small room. James crouched under the window to listen.

"Have you got the will?" Mrs. Evans asked.

"I've got it," replied the man.

"Good," said Mrs. Evans. "Drive into town and have it copied. I want to keep a copy out here in your house. When the time comes, I don't want to have to worry about getting the original out of his vault. Sometimes they come and lock up papers, and it can take for-

ever to get to the will. As my husband, you have an interest, too, you know."

Gary Painter was Mrs. Evans's second husband, then. But whose will did they have such an interest in?

There could be only one answer. The will had to be Stan Parker's. What was in it that could be of interest to Mrs. Evans and Mr. Painter? Were they to inherit money when Stan Parker died? Was Stan Parker in danger of dying soon, for some reason James didn't yet know?

He had to get back to the manor house. He could feel the danger, sense it as strongly as if he could touch it.

As James turned from the window, a shadow seemed to come right out of the walls of the small building. A second later, James felt pain—then nothing.

CHAPTER TEN

Skeletons in a Crypt

When James woke up, his head hurt and his temper flared. He could do nothing about his head. He calmed his temper with several deep breaths. James didn't like anger. It distorted judgment, and he needed good judgment now. He had awakened to find himself imprisoned in a damp underground dungeon from another time, another century. It was bitter cold.

"Blast!" said James to no one in particular.

Three of the dungeon's heavy stone walls had no openings at all. In the fourth, a small grating opened onto a passageway that was only a little less dark than the dungeon itself.

There was no way out.

"Blast!" James's voice rang along the stone passage.

"Blast to you, too! Holler again!"

87

It was Charlie. He had followed James's voice to the dungeon, and now he was just outside the grating. Charlie went nowhere without his fountain pen full of hydrochloric acid. The acid melted the lock in minutes, and James was out.

"Not bad, Charlie, thanks," said James, casually brushing a fleck of dirt from his perfectly pressed jeans. But he threw an affectionate arm around his friend in gratitude for his help.

"Where are the girls?" James asked.

"Getting sick," Charlie answered.

"Beg pardon?" James asked.

"Getting sick," Charlie repeated. "We found a room full of bones."

"The contents of those coffins?" James asked.

"Could be," said Charlie. "I'll have to do some tests in my lab. I've got a couple of samples here. I'll have to do some scrapings out of the coffins at the graveyard."

James nodded. He followed Charlie down the cold, damp, eerie stone passage to a room at the end. A room? It was a crypt! Stone sepulchers were piled to the ceiling. Headstones, inlaid with names and old dates, lay about the floor. On a massive marble sar-

cophagus in the center of the crypt were three skeletons partially covered with shreds of garments—leather boots, black suits, a dress of musty red silk.

Kathy stood there in the flickering light that cast eerie shadows through the crypt. She was grinning with what looked to James like the *risus sardonicus*, the "smile of death" that sometimes grips the face in the last horrible moments of life.

"Kathy, stop that!" Honey cried. "This is awful enough without you making that hideous face."

"Hideous is right," said Charlie.

Kathy, beautiful and vain about it, burst into tears. Whether it was because of hurt pride or relief at having the tension broken, she wasn't certain. Honey gave her friend a hug, as much to reassure herself as to comfort Kathy. The two of them pulled themselves together in the face of the ghoulish horror before them.

"Nothing awful here," said James. His cool, clinical manner calmed them all. "It's terrific. We've found, or rather you three have found, the contents of those coffins that were robbed. In a way, I'm relieved to have found them at Cornwall Crag."

"Why?" asked Kathy. "Doesn't it prove Mr. Parker is guilty?"

James shook his head. "There are others involved in whatever is going on here, not only Mr. Parker." He told his friends about the conversation he had overheard concerning Stan Parker's will. "And I don't yet know all I want to know about the lady, Dana Winter," he added.

"Then you're saying, James, that Mr. Parker may be the victim of a plot?" asked Honey.

"I am," James declared. "Charlie, if you've finished taking samples of these bones, we ought to go. School starts in three hours." One of Sam Star's rules was that work was never to interfere with school. James was absolutely scrupulous about obeying Sam's rules. If he weren't, he might lose the work he loved most in the world.

"Who do you think came at you from behind that house?" Honey wanted to know as they headed out of that awful passage and up into the main hall. "And who brought you here and left you in the dungeon?"

James shrugged and pulled on the navy windbreaker he had removed from the coyote and left on a chair earlier in the evening.

"Too many possibilities to guess," he said. "Even if Mr. Parker's in his rooms now, he could easily have left them for an hour or so earlier. Of course, it could have been either Mrs. Evans or Mr. Painter. It could even have been Dana Winter. There's Liz Evans to consider as well. And then," sighed James, "there's always my nemesis, ready to drop on my head whenever I need him least—Ratso Jones."

Charlie and Kathy had climbed into the Firebird and taken off like a shot. James and Honey went for the horses in the stable, where Band-Aid leaped for joy at being untethered.

"Sorry, old boy," said James, patting the black dog. "It was just too dangerous a night to have you along. But we're off home now. You can have an early-morning run to make up for a night in a strange stable."

The gallop back across the prairie, then down Old Cattle Road, made them all feel better.

They exchanged their horses for Honey's blue Honda at the Kawabata farm, and arrived back at the Star Agency with just enough time for breakfast before taking off for school.

They were halfway out the front door when the telephone rang in Sam's back office.

"James?" said Chief Adams. "I know how you feel about the guy, but I told you I'd stay out of it only if nothing else happened."

"What happened?" asked James.

"Capsized boat on Summertree River, up near the dam," said Chief Adams. "Near as I can figure, the boat was chased or pushed over the falls just under the bridge. James, the people who were in that boat are missing. We're searching now, dragging the river for bodies. It's still the full moon, James. Can you be absolutely sure your madman was under restraint last night—all night?"

CHAPTER ELEVEN

Dead or Alive?

By four o'clock that afternoon, only one person who'd been in the capsized boat had been found. Half of Kings Rock, including the entire police department and most of the fire department, was gathered under the bridge near the Summertree River dam.

"I don't know whether the waterfall or the crowd is more deafening," said the big, burly police chief as he watched from the bridge. "I can't hear myself think."

"Not much to think about, is there?" said Honey. "But at least we've got Mr. Hirsh out."

"Yes, and he'll be all right," said Chief Adams.

Honey, trying to keep her voice steady, said, "How long do you think little Johnny can last, chief?"

The boat had been found before dawn, but it wasn't till later in the morning that the police department found out who had been in it. Mrs. Hirsh had called the station to say that her husband and son had gone out camping the day before and hadn't returned; she was worried. When Chief Adams had asked whether they might have been on Summertree River in a small white-and-blue motorboat, Mrs. Hirsh stopped being worried. She became hysterical.

They had been dragging the river since dawn. So far they had found only Mr. Hirsh, jammed so tightly between two boulders that he had been unable to move, and barely able to keep his head above water.

Mr. Hirsh was now safe in Kings Rock Hospital.

Johnny Hirsh was still out there somewhere, either caught in the rapids upstream, lying farther downstream in the calm waters of the pool, or, like his father, pinned by boulders or fallen logs so he couldn't move.

The only question that mattered now was whether he was dead or alive.

"Over there," the chief called to the dragging team. "Down by the pool. Get the whole rig down by the pool. You know," he said more quietly, turning to Honey, "there's one thing I keep wondering."

"Yes, chief?" said Honey, flicking back her honey-colored hair.

"It's James I keep wondering about," said the chief. "Where's James Budd?"

James himself, handsome in a camel's hair jacket and oxford shirt, responded by coming up on the bridge just behind Honey and Chief Adams. He shook the chief's hand briefly, then lingered over hugging Honey.

"I've thought of something—someone, actually—that just might be able to help," said James.

He turned to present the powerful, handsome man beside him, a man whose hazel eyes gleamed with intelligence and concern as he took in the scene and the people around him. The caring that James had seen in the man early on was more evident than ever now.

"If you'll allow me," said Stan Parker. With a characteristic gesture, he ran a hand through his wild hair. As if changed by his new sense of purpose, his eyes, usually brooding, had come alive with an energy that even James hadn't suspected could be there.

Chief Adams turned to James. "I could have my commission taken away if I let Mr. Parker get involved here. He's the one suspected of tampering with the boat in the first place. And even if I bought your idea about his being harmless, James, the rest of the folks out there think he's a madman, a killer. If I don't take him in, they might turn on him themselves."

"Or you could give Mr. Parker a chance to vindicate himself," James said quietly.

Honey smiled. She'd never known anyone—not even Sam Star—to resist James Budd when he got like that.

"Right," said the chief quietly, after a long pause. "Go to it, Mr. Parker. We'd be grateful for any help at all right now. That little boy's been out there twelve hours or more, near as we can figure."

Without another word, Stan Parker stripped to the lightweight wet suit he had put on under his clothes. He had breathing apparatus and an underwater searchlight with him as well.

Just as quickly, James stripped down to similar gear.

"James!" Honey cried. But there was no stopping him. Stan Parker led the way as the two dived into the dark, treacherous waters of Summertree River. James followed Stan respectfully, knowing that with his experience in a wartime navy, he had mastered techniques that neither James nor anyone else in Kings Rock understood.

Stan Parker's powerful, slender body led James downstream, searching back and forth under the water far more thoroughly than the clumsy dragnets could possibly work.

They stayed underwater for long periods, their equipment equal to the task. James had always been quick of mind and body. But the powerful, energetic Stan Parker was more so. James followed Stan swiftly, parting and pushing and pulling boulders and weeds under the water and along the shore.

Every few hundred yards they surfaced— and faced a screaming crowd.

"He's going to kill my son the way he almost killed my husband," was the fiercest and loudest scream they heard.

"Get the madman out of the water!"

"He'll only make things worse. He's dangerous!"

"Should have been locked up years ago!"

"If he does find poor Johnny, he'll probably murder him!"

James touched Stan Parker's arm. The two submerged once more, without explanation, without reply.

Ten minutes later, Stan Parker found the small body.

It was covered with leaves, wedged between the branches of a fallen tree, and it had just begun to slip into the water. In another five minutes it would have slipped all the way in. If not for Stan Parker, the body might never have been found. If not for Stan Parker, the body might never have breathed again.

Faster than James had ever seen anyone move, Stan Parker bent back one branch sufficiently to loosen the tree's grip on the small boy. The minute the child was loose, Stan had him up on the riverbank, flat on the moss under the yellowing willows. With skills learned during the nightmare of his life, Stan Parker breathed life back into Johnny Hirsh's body.

With his first deep gasps, the boy began to cry.

"Good," said Stan. "Cry, child. Cry away the terror, and gasp in the oxygen for the heart and brain."

James watched the miracle of lifesaving

before him, then looked away. He preferred never to be overcome by any emotion whatever.

The two, with Stan Parker carrying the child, walked back upriver to where Johnny's mother was waiting with the crowd. The people were still screaming as they watched James and Stan approach. When they saw what Stan was carrying, the noise stopped as if it had been cut with a knife.

"It's all right, Mrs. Hirsh," said James, stepping forward to reassure the mother. "Johnny's alive. Mr. Stanley Parker of Cornwall Crag saved your son's life."

Mrs. Hirsh held out her arms. She took her child, pressed him to her, was silent for a moment, then screamed out.

"You think I'll thank you? You think I'll thank the madman who hurt my child in the first place, just because he's tried to undo his harm now?"

James watched the big man bow his head in the face of the hysterical mother's attack, accepting guilt, absorbing her pain along with his own.

James had never been so near hitting a woman in his life.

CHAPTER TWELVE

Honey Is Missing

The golden light of the late afternoon waned as James drove a silent Stan Parker back to Cornwall Crag. The man, whose suffering had briefly been eased by his ability to help, had once again been banished by public opinion to the prison his home had become.

James pulled into the cobbled driveway in front of the stone manor house. Stan Parker got out of the car slowly, heavily.

"Will you be coming in?" he asked somewhat hesitantly. He seemed unwilling to impose his company on James.

"Of course," said James with no hesitation at all.

Mrs. Evans greeted them with a smile, rubbing floury hands on her apron. "Will you have tea, gentlemen?" she asked.

"Mrs. Evans is English," Stan reminded

James. "Tea means sandwiches, cake, biscuits with butter and honey and four kinds of jam, sometimes cold chicken, and always two kinds of dessert."

"I'm hungry enough," said James. "It's been a hard afternoon."

"It has," agreed Stan as he led the way toward the fireplace in the living room.

The gloomy furniture and dark draperies were as depressing, James thought, as the barren trees, the wilderness of the gardens where nothing grew but weeds, the mists that clung like a shroud to the stone towers of the ancient house.

"There hasn't been the feeling of life here for a long time," said Stan Parker, as if reading James's thoughts.

James felt the tremendous weariness of the man. He veiled his compassion for a moment to ask, "Why have you given up, sir? I know the question sounds brutal, considering what the world has been handing you. But still . . ."

"Quite right, young man." A woman's voice rang across the room like a bell on a clear day. "I've asked Stan that a thousand times."

James could see at a glance the bravery, the effort, the hope in the woman's face. He sensed how hard it was for her to come here.

Even dressed in ordinary clothes—a soft gray sweater and skirt—Dana Winter was astoundingly beautiful, James thought. He noticed that Stan Parker thought so, too. For a moment, Stan and Dana looked at each other with such love, such longing, that James felt he was intruding, and looked away.

Dana Winter gently touched Stan Parker's wild hair, then sat across from Stan to hear about the afternoon's events. James told more of the story than Stan did. Dana Winter understood instantly what had happened when they'd brought the boy back.

"I mustn't ever leave here," Stan Parker cried out. "There is something so wrong with me, I contaminate whatever I touch."

"You saved the life of that boy," said Dana Winter. "If you would let me live with you and love you, you might even save my life— our lives—before it's too late."

"I'm not fit for an ordinary life. You know that, Dana. You know the ghastly secret of my—my attacks," answered Stan, who now strode about the room in anguish. "I hurt whatever I touch, Dana. I love you with all my heart. Do you think, even for a minute, that I would risk hurting you, whom I love most in the world, with this sickness of mine, this thing that happens to me? I want you to go," he finished.

But only part of him wanted his lady to go, James felt. The other part of him longed for her as cornfields long for the sun.

"We've done this to him, you know," Dana Winter cried out passionately. "All of us, we have our part in what happens to the young men who fight in the wars of the world. We talk about peace, but we cheer our soldiers on, make heroes of boys who kill. We supply the emotional ammunition. And then we tell the men it's they who are wrong, they who have done dreadful things. We're all responsible, but it's the men like Stan who bear the scars."

A strident voice cut through Dana Winter's words. It was accompanied by the rattling entrance of the tea cart.

"Are you here again, disturbing my patient? He's always so upset after your visits, it's a wonder you keep coming round like you do." Mrs. Evans's words were clipped as she busied herself with setting out cups and pouring tea.

"Shall I stay?" asked Dana Winter quietly. "Shall I go?"

James saw that it wasn't Mrs. Evans Dana was talking to.

"Go," said Stan Parker. He sat down in the fireside chair, burying his face in his hands. "It's better if you go."

Dana Winter rose quietly.

James followed her through the double doors to the great hall. "I don't want to lose you in the mists again," he said. "Where can I find you if I think you're needed? And I do think you'll be needed, Miss Winter, and soon."

Dana pressed a card with a telephone number and address into James's hand. It was unlike James to show affection for anyone other than Sam or Honey, but he touched Dana Winter's shoulder for a second in promise, in a shared hope.

"I'll call you every day, whatever happens," said James.

The woman's eyes filled with gratitude, and she left.

"James," called Mrs. Evans from the downstairs study. "James Budd. It's the telephone. It's for you."

"James," cried Kathy Howard, when James picked up the telephone. "It's Honey. I can't find her anywhere. She's not at home, she's not with any of our friends, I couldn't find her in town, she's not out at the Kawabata farm. Her Honda is in her driveway. I don't know what else to do, where else to look, James."

James took a deep breath. There were many things one could mess with in James Budd's life without risking very much. Honey Mack wasn't one of them.

For the second time that day, James had the urge to strike, to hurt.

CHAPTER THIRTEEN

Ratso Plays a Part

As James sped through the September evening, the last pink-gold rays of the sunset faded. So did his patience. By the time James had raced across the northern end of town and down Station Road, he didn't care how he got Ratso Jones to talk. But he was going to make Ratso talk.

James felt every one of his strong, well-trained muscles respond to the need to find Honey, and to find her before anyone could harm her.

The Firebird raced past the railway station and south a few hundred feet until James was across from the Rat Gang's shack. From the yellow glow in the windows, James knew that Ratso was there. James jumped the car over the railway tracks and practically rammed it into the shack wall.

He flung open the door.

"You don't knock anymore?" said Ratso.

The thin, mean-faced leader of the Rat Gang half rose from the rickety table where he and Tom and Sharky had been playing cards by the light of a naked bulb.

"Where is she? Where's Honey Mack?" said James coldly and slowly. His threatening tone conveyed every possible shade of meaning. "Nothing vile goes on in this town without your knowing something about it, Ratso. Nothing criminal happens without your having something to do with it, even if it's just picking up a couple of bucks to keep your mouth shut."

James took a few steps forward, assuming a position only someone familiar with kung fu would have recognized. He was ready to attack. If Ratso didn't answer James within seconds, James's left hand would execute a tiger claw on Ratso's throat, while his right would rip Ratso's forearm, leaving it useless.

"Hey," said Tom, getting up from his chair. "We don't know nothing. We're just sitting here, minding our own business, playing cards."

"Yeah," said Sharky. "Yeah, that's all."

James froze both of them with a look.

"Well?" said James to Ratso.

Ratso Jones wasn't stupid. He knew better than to make small talk and tempt James into using every martial arts lesson he had ever learned.

"Well," Ratso began, "while you and the madman were getting the kid out of the river, Honey went nosing around up at Cornwall Crag. Some lady up there had got word that I could be useful about certain things. She called me. I went up there to get Honey out of the way."

James's black eyes glittered with menace. Ratso raised both hands in surrender.

"I swear, James, I swear that by the time I got there, there wasn't any Honey. That housekeeper, Mrs. Evans, she told me that Honey had left already. So I don't know who called, or who got to Honey. I don't, James, and that's a fact," said Ratso.

Ratso had begun to eye a pile of heavy chain that lay coiled in a corner of the shack. James's foot shot out so fast, it connected with Ratso's jaw before Ratso could blink at the chain one more time. Ratso stood up shakily and spat out a tooth.

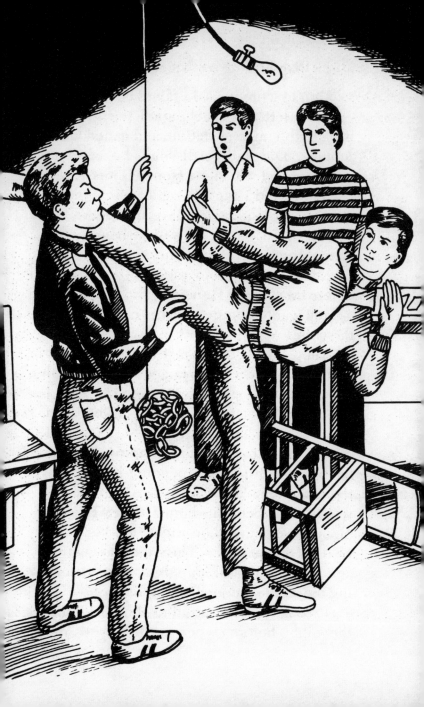

"Don't be funny," said James coldly.

James left the shack, sped the Firebird back to the railway station, and called Chief Adams. "Did Kathy call you?" he asked. "I told her to let you know Honey is missing."

"She called," said the chief. "I've got an APB out for Honey. You have any ideas?"

"Yes," said James. "I've just been to see Ratso Jones. He told me something he doesn't know he told me. I think I know where they've got Honey."

"You want a couple of patrol cars?" offered the chief.

"Keep the APB out just in case. But no, thanks, no cars," said James. "Check with you later."

"Hey, where are you going?" asked Chief Adams.

But James had already hung up. He was back in the Firebird, speeding back across town and up Old Cattle Road to exactly where he'd been an hour before. The full moon was rising. The night was clear and cold out on the plains. The wind was gusting, agitating the air as if something were disturbing the whole mood of the night.

He took the old, rutted road he had taken the night before, when he followed Mrs.

Evans. In twenty minutes he was at Gary Painter's house.

James was nearly positive that what Honey had been "nosing around" for while everyone else was down at the river was Stan Parker's will. James was also nearly positive that she had been caught and taken here for safekeeping.

But being nearly positive wasn't the same as seeing his girl safe and alive. James crashed the door in.

"Thank God," he whispered.

He untied the ropes from Honey's wrists, then the rope around her waist that bound her to the bedstead.

"And thank *you*, James," said Honey, burying her face in his neck.

He stroked the long, honey-blond hair. "Later, baby," he said softly. "We'll hold each other later. Right now . . ."

"I know," said Honey. "There's work to do. To answer the first question you're going to ask, I don't know. Someone came up behind me, knocked me out, and the next thing I knew, I was here."

James called Chief Adams from Mrs. Jarko's cottage. "She's safe," said James. "I've got her here."

"Good, but call me back in an hour," said the chief. "By then I'll have news from the lab about the boat."

"Right," said James.

As he started the Firebird, he turned to Honey. "Do you mind if we go to Kings Rock for an hour or so?" he asked. "I think we both need some fresh air."

Honey smiled. "Let's pick up some coffee and sandwiches at The Hut and have supper under that glorious moon."

Half an hour later, they were once again on their way out of town, but this time to a place that meant peace.

Kings Rock was up Old Cattle Road, just beyond the scrub oak. James could see it from his bedroom window, hear the wind sweep and moan across it from the mountain pass. It had the color, the roar, and in bad weather the treachery of any angry lion, the king of beasts—hence its name. Few people went there at all. No one could follow James when he came up into the hills from the prairies.

As he led Honey up the craggy clefts to-night, he shook his dark mane as a lion might shake its golden one. Then he turned to Honey.

"I was going to wait until Stan Parker cleared himself. I was going to wait until Mrs. Evans hanged herself with her own behavior. I was going to wait at least until Sam got home," he said. "But Mr. Parker has had enough, heaven knows you've had enough, and so have I. Let's go."

An hour and a half later, when James called, Chief Adams said, "James, that boat accident was no accident. The outboard motor had been tampered with. Someone wanted those two people to drown. And James, there's something else. A man over in Spalding was found hanging from his own living room rafters. His neighbors got to him just in time to cut him down. He didn't do it himself. He says he was attacked from behind, never saw his attacker. And James," the chief added, "when I called Mr. Parker to ask him if he knew anything, he admitted to all of it, everything that's happened in the last five days. He says he did it all."

"Can you give me some time before you take him in?" James asked.

Like Sam, the chief trusted James.

"Twenty-four hours," the chief answered.

CHAPTER FOURTEEN

Sam on the Scene

"He's admitted to everything," James told Honey as he hung up.

They were in front of the fireplace in the leather-and-brass living room.

"Call him," said Honey. "We can't just let him suffer with that alone."

James picked up the phone again. The soft lamplight, the warmth of the fire, the ripe Brie cheese, the crusty French bread, the slightly chilled Perrier, and the loveliness of his girl leaning her head against his knee— all would have to wait. James could not abandon Stan Parker.

"Mr. Parker?" said James, when he had gotten through to Cornwall Crag.

"Yes. Is it James Budd?" came the weary voice.

"How could you admit to all that stuff?" said James. His tone was angry, but his anger wasn't at the man.

"They may be right after all," said Stan. "I'm truly mad—and I may be growing more dangerous all the time. I've caused more violence during this full moon than ever before. James, it may be better for everyone if I'm put away."

"I have one question," said James. "What are the terms of your will?"

Honey sat up straight. She put her ear to the phone, so that she, too, could hear Stan Parker's reply.

"Simply that in the event of either my death or my confinement to some institution where I shall be deemed incurably mad, those who have cared for me all these years, namely Mrs. Evans and Mr. Painter, shall inherit all of my estate—money, lands, all of it. It was the only way, James, that I could assure myself that I would be well guarded and would do no harm during my attacks."

"Could you go nowhere, do nothing, until tomorrow afternoon?" said James. "After all, the Star Agency represents you, and it wouldn't be fair to us to walk out on what is now our case as well as yours."

"Fair is fair," said Stan, and James could almost hear his smile. It was the smile of someone who simply didn't care any longer.

"Hang on," said James. "We'll be there around four o'clock tomorrow."

James heard a slight click before he replaced the receiver.

"We've been listened in on up at Cornwall Crag," said James. "And we'll be waited for tomorrow."

James put in a call to Sam Star.

"Need you," said James. "No nonsense."

When James and Honey walked into the office after school on Thursday, the small, wiry, sharp-eyed man who sat on the edge of the desk, one hand on the phone, the other making notes in a pad, looked up at them and grinned from under his gray fedora.

"Hi," he said.

Honey wrapped her arms around Sam Star and gave him a kiss that made him blush with embarrassment and pleasure.

James gazed with equal pleasure at the man he admired most in the world. Sam gazed back at James with absolute joy and pride.

"Now that we have gotten through a disgusting moment," said Sam, still beaming, "tell me every detail about The Madman at Cornwall Crag. I'm assuming, Honey, that that's the name of the case."

The three conferred for half an hour. James outlined his plan. He had to find the copy of Stan Parker's will, and he had to find it in Mr. Painter's house to convict Mrs. Evans and Mr. Painter. James planned on going out to Cornwall Crag on horseback for a silent approach, and on bringing Band-Aid in case of trouble. He wanted Stan Parker to accompany them out to Gary Painter's shack, to shock a confession from the culprits.

"Sounds good," said Sam. "But I'm going to let Frank Adams in on this. I was just on the phone with him. He says people in the towns around here are pretty angry—angry enough for a mob scene if we don't solve this one soon."

James nodded. "It'll be over by tonight. If the plan works, we'll have enough evidence to build an airtight case."

"Take care," said Sam.

"We will," said Honey.

They were off. James collected Band-Aid from next door, let him jump into the Firebird, and took off for the Kawabata farm to get the horses.

Tad Kawabata was waiting for them at the stables with the black stallion and Honey's favorite roan. James and Honey were on their way in a flash, leading a spare mount for Stan Parker. Charlie Alda had rigged their jackets with hidden pockets full of small electronic equipment as well as fake pens and lighters carrying chemicals they might need.

The forty-five-minute ride in the late September afternoon was gorgeous under the wide Nebraska skies. The leaves were growing as gold as the autumn sunset, and the prairie glowed beneath the reddening clouds.

It was only as they approached the stone manor of Cornwall Crag that everything seemed to turn gray again. Clouds and mists were paler here, the trees were more barren, the ground was harsh and cold as the mood of the ancient house.

"Good afternoon," said Mrs. Evans, her

manner as cheerful as ever. "How nice. Just in time for tea. Mr. Parker is by the fire in the downstairs drawing room. A bit broody, he is. He'll be glad of a visit."

Were her eyes a shade more watchful, a touch more alert? James wondered. Was it Mrs. Evans who had listened in on the telephone yesterday? Or Mr. Painter, or Liz? Or even the woman in white, Dana Winter?

"How nice to see you, James," came the playful greeting of Liz Evans, her dark curls bouncing, her dark eyes teasing James as she crossed the huge hall. "You, too, of course, Honey Mack," she added, and went laughing off into the kitchen as if she had hidden some mad joke below stairs.

"Lunatic asylum, this place," Honey whispered. "I mean, if Stan Parker wasn't mad before, this place and these people would have done him in anyway."

"And may well have," said James. He led the way into the drawing room.

"Mr. Parker, do you have time for a ride with us before Mrs. Evans brings us tea?" James asked. "We've come on horseback especially to take you out for some air."

Stan Parker looked up as if any physical activity at all, much less a ride across the prairie, were perfectly meaningless. But he had agreed not to question James. "If you wish," he said.

Soon the three, accompanied by Band-Aid, were cantering gently against the rising wind. The moorlike prairie, oddly marshy for this part of Nebraska, was treacherous. But James had counted on Stan Parker knowing his land, and he and Honey followed him.

"How do you know I'm not leading you into a bog somewhere?" said Stan dryly. "I mean, with my reputation, you could end up in quicksand and never be seen again."

"Stop that, sir," said James sharply.

The mists rose from the boggy ground and curled around the horses' hooves. Their view was obscured for a moment or two—just long enough so that the horses reared in fright when a man suddenly appeared before them.

The three good riders were able to calm their horses. But not for long. The man raised a bullwhip into the air and spun it, whirled it, cracked it above their heads.

The horses reared again.

"Get down," said Mr. Painter, for the man

with the bullwhip was Stan Parker's gar-
dener-chauffeur. "Now!"

The three managed to quiet their horses
and dismount.

"Come forward," said Mr. Painter. "I've got
my net. I'm good with my net and my whip.
There's no escape, not without more pain
than you can imagine. Do as I say. Come
forward."

"Obey him," said James sharply.

As sharply, he gave Band-Aid a command.
Dog and horses took off, as first a net, then a
club, came down on James, Honey, and Stan
Parker.

CHAPTER FIFTEEN

Locked in the Crypt

James returned to consciousness slowly, in pain, and imprisoned. In the dim light he could see the headstones, the marble vaults, and the heavy grille of the crypt of Cornwall Crag.

"Blast!" James muttered. The damp air and the sensation of waking among the dead weren't pleasant.

"Blast is right!" came another voice.

"Honey! How are you?" said James, relieved that he had company, but sorry that Honey was suffering so much during this case.

In the dark, the two investigators found and investigated each other, from scalp wounds to battered knees. Lightly and skillfully, James touched all the parts that might have been injured as they were netted, clubbed, and thrown unconscious into the dark, underground crypt.

"We'll live?" Honey asked.

"We'll live," James announced.

"Thank God you're both all right," came a resonant voice from deep among the sepulchers.

"Mr. Parker, you're down here, too!" said Honey.

Before Stan Parker had a chance to answer, there was a sound from the passageway.

Light, from an old-fashioned flaming torch thrust into a holding ring in the stone wall just outside the grille, suddenly illuminated the crypt.

"Mrs. Evans, what in heaven's name is going on? What are we doing here?" Mr. Parker demanded. "At least you've come, Mrs. Evans. Have you got the keys? Be kind enough to get us out quickly. Our young detective friends have surely had enough of the goings-on around here."

Mrs. Evans, however, did not move. "You are exactly where I want you, Mr. Parker," she said. "After all the trouble Mr. Painter and I have had getting all three of you down here, why on earth should I let you out?"

Stan Parker was shocked. But James was not at all surprised.

"You provided in your will," he said to Stan, "that in the event of your death or certified insanity, Mrs. Evans and Mr. Painter would inherit Cornwall Crag, lock, stock, barrel, and income."

James came forward to glare at Mrs. Evans through the heavy grille. "Mrs. Evans has just been hurrying the matter along, isn't that right?" he said. "It made no difference to her whether they got you on a charge of criminal insanity or whether she got you herself—just so long as you were got, Mr. Parker. Right, Mrs. Evans?" He glowered at the woman, who loomed large and menacing in the flickering torchlight.

"It can't matter now that you know, James Budd," said Mrs. Evans sardonically. "You'll never tell, because you'll never leave this crypt alive. But you're right, of course. Mr. Painter and I robbed the graves. You even caught Mr. Painter going back for a scarf, remember? And we set the barns on fire—poor Liz nearly found us out that night, and we had to put her out for a bit, I'm afraid. But that was just one more thing we could blame on Mr. Parker. It was we who stole Mrs. Jarko's rabbits, who set the animal trap, tampered with the boat, and strung up that man. We even had to bang you and Miss Mack about a little from time to time, when you got too close. It was Mr. Painter who ruined the brakes and the headlights on your car, for instance, in case you were wondering."

Mrs. Evans gave a small, scornful laugh. "It was nothing to convince Mr. Parker he'd done all those awful things," she went on. "We simply drugged him, told him he'd had another blackout, then told him what he'd done. He was always ready to assume the guilt for anything. We hired you, of course, to make our part seem quite innocent, as if we were defending Mr. Parker all the way. We did all that, and I'd have done more if I'd had to. I've taken care of the rich all my life, and I'm bloody sick of it. When Mr. Parker fell into my life, it was like a sign to me that I didn't have to be a poor servant any longer. Make the world think he's crazy and violent, so they'll either kill him or lock him up—and me and mine will be set for life."

Mrs. Evans leaned forward. "When Mr. Parker left the asylum, I knew he was cured. But he was still unsure of his strength, and with the help of drugs and some made-up stories about the full moon, we could play on his old guilts, Mr. Painter and I. Mr. Parker has been perfectly sane for years—he's just never had a chance to find that out. But you can be sure no one else is going to find that out, either. Not when Cornwall Crag can belong to me!"

Mrs. Evans's face was no longer kind or cheerful. It was twisted with greed, with evil delight in her own vengeance.

James started to say something, to protest, but Stan interrupted him.

"Let her be," said Stan in his gentle voice. "She's no worse than any of us, only untaught."

"Glad you're in a charitable mood," said Mrs. Evans. "You're a good man, Mr. Parker. I bear you no personal ill will. Good-by."

"Good-by?" yelled Honey. "Good-by?"

"Yes," said Mrs. Evans, turning away and taking the torch with her. "I'll have no trouble convincing the authorities that the madman killed you and took his own life in a suicidal fit. Say your prayers, then. I'll be back shortly with Mr. Painter and his hypodermic needle. A shot each, three air bubbles through the heart, a quick pain, and then it's done. That's all that's needed."

Without another word, Mrs. Evans marched down the passageway.

James tapped his jacket pocket. "Got all that right here on tape," he said with satisfaction.

"Terrific," said Honey. "The dead will talk after all. We'll live on through James Budd's microcassette."

"I don't plan to be dead," said James. "Or to see my friends die, either. I could never forgive myself for not getting my girl out of here. And Miss Winter would never forgive me for not getting her husband-to-be out of here."

A flicker of a smile lifted Stan Parker's mouth.

"At least she'll know I'm innocent," he said. "At least I can give her that much after all these loving and loyal years. Thank God for that, James, that Dana and I know I didn't commit all that evil. Thank God, and thank *you*!"

"Not yet," said James. "No thanks to me till we're out."

"Soon?" said Honey. "Anything I can do?"

"Soon," said James. "And you can hold this."

From an inside pocket, James produced

what appeared to be a short, black magician's stick.

"Terrific," said Honey. "We're about to be buried alive in this old crypt, and he's going to do magic tricks."

"In a way," said James. "Only they're Charlie's tricks, not mine."

James took a grappling hook from another pocket, retrieved the black stick from Honey, attached the two, and gave the stick a sharp shake. The whole became an extremely strong wrecking tool.

When this tool was ready, James took out a fountain pen filled with hydrochloric acid, applied the acid to a few key places on the grille, attached the grappling hook to the bars, and yelled, "Get back into the farthest part of this crypt you can reach."

Stan took hold of Honey and got her safely into an empty sarcophagus. Then he came back to give James a hand. Three minutes later, the two men brought down the heavy iron grille that had been rooted in the ancient stone for centuries.

"About time," said Stan Parker, clearly enjoying the destruction of this monument to death. "Let the dead bury the dead," he added. "It's time for the living."

Their glee kept the three of them going as they ran through the passageway and out into the front hall of the manor. There they came to a halt, the joy leaking out of their toes as they faced net and needle.

Mr. Painter was there, holding in his right hand the huge net he was so adept at throwing, and in his left the hypodermic he was so adept at shooting.

"Now!" James called out sharply, as the net billowed over them like a great cloud.

Honey was used to following James's body signals. Stan Parker's war experience had taught him to be equally swift and responsive.

James headed for the stairs, and the other two followed, just barely missing being caught in the spidery net.

"After them!" Mrs. Evans called out from below. "Gary Painter, you get after them. Don't let years go to waste. Chase them up!"

Gary Painter obeyed.

"You lead," James yelled.

Stan Parker, his joy in discovering his own innocence and sanity giving him added strength, grabbed Honey in his arms and led the way up a set of narrow stone stairs, nearly hidden in the wall of the old house. The stairs wound higher and higher. At the top was a narrow door. As Stan Parker held Honey, James rammed open the door with his shoulder, and the three burst out onto the stone ramparts of the turreted roof.

The September night was glorious. The three of them were free.

"No one knows about those stairs," said Stan, "and there's a secret way down as well."

There was a noise behind them.

"You think we haven't explored every inch of this house over the years?" said Mrs. Evans. "Now, Gary Painter! We'll push them now. We can still blame it on the madman!"

CHAPTER SIXTEEN

Future Plans
— and Pillows

"It certainly was a nice feeling, seeing you and Band-Aid and Miss Winter coming across that roof," said James the following Sunday evening.

He was carrying a supper tray into the cozy leather-and-brass living room, which was alive with firelight and the two people he loved most in the world. In their honor, he had made dinner himself. On the tray were curried fish, a light salad, an excellent loaf of bread, two bottles of Perrier, and coffee. He placed the tray on the large, low coffee table in front of the fireplace, poured the Perrier into three glasses, and took his place next to Honey on the sofa, across from Sam Star. James sighed with contentment, one hand on his Perrier, the other on his girl's knee.

"Glad to oblige," said Sam. He gazed with

affection at his adopted son, more relieved than he cared to admit that James was safe. "Good idea, sending Band-Aid back for me. It was fortunate, though, that Dana Winter, who said she could always sense intuitively when Stan Parker was in danger, was waiting for me downstairs. Might have had trouble locating those hidden stairs without her. We'd seen you on the roof, but I'd have had a hard time getting up there without her."

"It's nice that they're finally together, finally able to share their lives without all that dreadful fear to haunt them," said Honey. "How awful to spend your own life terrified to love the woman you love because you're afraid of your own insanity, afraid you might even hurt her."

Sam pushed back the gray fedora, put his feet up, and grinned.

"It's nice *you* don't worry, Honey," said Sam, "you being in love with a lunatic yourself."

James Budd leaned back comfortably and grinned at Sam. "Adored elder, I'll thank you to keep your opinions to yourself and leave me to keep my girl to myself."

"Leave you is right," said Sam Star.

Sam reached into his pocket and pulled out an envelope. An airline ticket wafted down onto James's chest.

"That's for Edwards Air Force Base in California, plane leaving Loden Airport Friday after school," said Sam. "There's something I need you to do on this NASA case, this *Secret of Operation Brain* I'm working on. Meet you there Friday evening. I'm taking off right after dinner tonight."

"Before you take off," said Honey, "tell us what's going to happen to Mrs. Evans and Mr. Painter, to say nothing of poor Liz."

"Well, it is their luck, and I mean only their luck," said Sam, "that nobody actually got killed with all their messing around. So they're not up for murder or even manslaughter. But they'll get years for everything from felony assault for the hanged man and Johnny Hirsh, to defamation of character for all the harm done to Stanley Parker. Not to mention every swindle charge on the books, mental cruelty, and all that. They'll also be sued for opened graves, burned barns, wrecked boats, and whatever else."

"I have a whatever else," said James. "The kidnapping and bumping around of my girl and my Watson."

"Yes, Sherlock," said Sam Star. "But I admit you have a point."

"How about Liz Evans?" said Honey. "Will she be all right? I think James rather fancied her."

Honey curled into James's shoulder and fluttered her eyelashes in imitation of the beautiful dark-haired girl.

"Dana and Stan Parker volunteered to look after her for a bit," said Sam. "She'll be all right with them, I think."

"And available," James Budd said with a straight face.

Sam Star grinned and went to the kitchen for more coffee—and to avoid the sudden punching and throwing of pillows that had broken out on the living room sofa.

ABOUT THE AUTHOR

Dale Carlson has been writing stories since she was eight years old. She is the author of more than forty books for young people, including three ALA Notable Books: *The Mountain of Truth, The Human Apes,* and *Girls Are Equal Too.* Her book *Where's Your Head?* won a Christopher Award.

Ms. Carlson lives in New York City.

THE JAMES BUDD MYSTERIES

1. The Mystery of the Madman at Cornwall Crag
2. The Secret of Operation Brain
3. The Mystery of the Lost Princess
4. The Mystery of Galaxy Games